Steph and the Sea Sprite

by Damian Harvey and Lucy Semple

W
FRANKLIN WATTS
LONDON•SYDNEY

Steph and the Sea Sprite

Contents

Chapter 1

After School

The last day of school seemed to be dragging on forever. Steph kept looking at the clock but the hands didn't seem to be moving at all, as though time was standing still. When finally the bell rang for the end of the school day, Steph rushed to pack her things away.

"Looks like you're in a hurry, Steph," said Mr Jones. "You must have something important planned for this evening."

"Not really sir," Steph replied, stuffing books into her bag. "I'm just meeting some friends for a kickabout on the beach."

Mr Jones raised his eyebrows and shook his head sadly. "It's a shame you won't be taking your football then."

Steph groaned. She'd forgotten all about that. Her football had been confiscated at lunchtime.

"It wasn't my fault," Steph replied. "I didn't mean to break the window."

Mr Jones nodded. "I know," he sighed. "It's never your fault. But don't worry, your ball will still be here for you on Monday."

Steph pulled a face but she knew there was no point arguing with Mr Jones. Hopefully, one of her friends would bring a ball for once.

Steph headed straight for the beach. When she got there, she called in at the Sand Dune Café where Mum worked.

"Hi, Steph," Mr Arnold, the café owner, called from behind the counter. "Your mum said you'd be coming in so I got these ready for you." He had put some snacks and drinks into a bag for her.

"Thanks, Mr Arnold," Steph smiled. "That's really kind of you."

"Make sure you all put your rubbish in the bin," Mum called from the kitchen.

Steph rolled her eyes and grinned. "Don't worry," she said. "Of course I will!"

Steph picked up the bag of goodies and headed outside. It was a warm evening and there were lots of people on the beach. Everyone was making the most of the nice weather, and children were building sandcastles while their parents sat reading or chatting.

Out at sea, a couple of windsurfers were gliding across the waves on their boards. There was even someone riding a horse along the shoreline.

Steph looked around for her friends. She found them sitting on the sand, watching a bearded old man who was making something out of driftwood and bits of rubbish.

Giving her friends a wave, she ran over to join them.

"Has anyone brought a ball?" asked Steph. "Mine's been confiscated."

"No ball?" moaned Noah, pulling a face.

"Sorry, no," Steph replied. Then she held up the carrier bag. "But I have got these."

"Cool!" said Amir. "Who needs a ball when you've got goodies?"

Natalie took charge and shared the goodies out between them. They stuffed everything into their pockets, then Noah grabbed the empty plastic carrier bag.

Chapter 2

A Bit of Fun

"Watch this!" Noah took the bag by its handles and held it above his head. Then he started to run along the sand, the bag filling with air as he went.

Just before he reached the shoreline, Noah let go of the bag. The breeze caught it and lifted it. It soared high into the air like a kite.

"Look at it go," he cried.

"That's cool!" laughed Natalie. "Wish we had some more."

Not everyone thought it was cool, though. The old man with the beard called over to them. "Put your rubbish in the bin," he said. "Do not leave it on the beach."

Steph could feel her face turning red, even though it was Noah who had done something wrong, and not her.

"Oh, just ignore him," said Noah, sneering. "Some people

don't know how to have fun."

"Come on," said Amir. "Let's move along the beach.

He won't bother us there."

As the four friends walked along the sand, Noah did

impressions of the old man to make them laugh.

"What a strange old man he is," Natalie said,

emptying the last of her crisps into her mouth. She took

out a drink and let the crisp packet fall on the sand.

Steph saw what Natalie had done and winced.

She turned and saw the old man glaring at them.

Steph popped a sweet into her mouth, making sure

she stuffed the wrapper into her pocket. She didn't want

to get shouted at again.

"Come on!" said Noah. "I know what we can do."

As she followed the others, Steph checked to see if the old man was still watching them. Thankfully, he was busy with his pile of driftwood and rubbish.

Up ahead, Natalie had finished the last of her drink. She scooped some sand into the bottle and then threw it across the water. The bottle landed with a splash and bobbed about in the waves.

"Let's have a competition to see who can throw their bottle the furthest," she said. "The weight of the sand makes it go further."

"Is that the best you can do?" said Noah. "I bet I could beat that."

Half-filling his bottle with sand, Noah took a run-up before letting go of his bottle.

They all watched as Noah's bottle flew high into the air, and past Natalie's.

"Beat that, Amir!" boasted Noah.

"I haven't finished mine," Amir replied, putting his bottle in his pocket.

"My turn!" said Steph. "This is how you do it."

She was about to throw when she felt some kind of force stopping her. "Hey!" she cried. "Let go!"

Expecting it to be one of the others, Steph was shocked to see the bearded old man standing behind her.

Chapter 3

The Sea Sprite

Steph's heart was pounding in her chest and her face burned with embarrassment. Something was gripping her wrist, but the man was not touching her.

As she stared at her raised hand, the feeling gradually faded. Keeping hold of the bottle, she slowly lowered her arm to her side.

Steph looked at the old man. "We were just having a laugh," she explained. "Weren't we," she said, turning to her friends.

But no one answered her. No one spoke.

No one even moved. It was as if they were frozen to the spot.

Natalie had her hands on her hips and her mouth was open, but there were no words coming out.

Looking round, Steph realised that everything on the beach had completely stopped. One of the windsurfers was in mid-air, frozen whilst performing a trick. On the beach, two children stood motionless with buckets and spades. In the air, two gulls had been halted as they dived down to snatch a dropped sandwich. And not a wave was moving on the sea. It was as if time had stood still.

This was really weird ...

"You were going to throw that bottle into the sea,"
said the old man. "I had to stop you."

Steph looked at the mysterious old man and wondered
who he could be. It was hard to tell how old he was.
His eyes were as blue as the sea on a summer's day.
His grey beard was long and tangled, with strands of
seaweed running through it. And despite looking old,
his body seemed strong and powerful.

"It's only a bottle," she said. "What's it got to do with you?"

"I am a sea sprite," said the man. "I am as old as the oceans
and have had many names, but you may call me Boreal.
Now come with me. There are many things I wish
to show you."

"What things?" Steph frowned.

Without replying, Boreal raised his hands into the air.
As he did, a cloud of sand lifted, swirled and whirled
around them.

Steph imagined it was like being in the centre of
a hurricane.

When the swirling subsided a little, Steph found herself
in the same place on the beach. But her friends were
no longer beside her.

Further along the beach, Steph could see a group of people eating, drinking and laughing. Next to them were huge sacks of rubbish. She spotted Amir amongst them.

"Hey!" Steph shouted, waving. "Amir!"

"He cannot see you," explained Boreal. "You are not really here. This is tomorrow."

"Tomorrow?" frowned Steph. "Will I be here too?"

"That will be up to you," Boreal replied. "I want to show you the rubbish they have collected."

"Wow! That's a lot of rubbish," said Steph. "But it's nothing to do with me, is it? I didn't drop anything."

Boreal's eyes flashed angrily for a moment, then the swirling sands rose up again.

Chapter 4

Into the Future

Immediately, Steph could tell that things on the beach were now different. The sun was still shining but there was hardly anyone in sight. In the distance, she could see a man walking his dog. Two women were jogging across the sands, but apart from that, the beach was deserted. Today, there were no children building sandcastles and nobody was windsurfing. Though it was hardly surprising that the beach was empty. The shoreline was completely covered with rubbish.

"Where are we now?" asked Steph.

"This is the future," Boreal explained. "Only a few years in the future, but look — see how different it is."

Steph nodded. "It's a mess," she said, and started walking along the shoreline. There were plastic bottles, pieces of rope and fishing nets, tin cans, and all sorts of junk.

Then Steph spotted something moving a little way ahead of them. "What's that?" she asked. "Right at the edge of the water."

When they reached it, Steph realised it was a seagull.

It had become tangled in a piece of netting and was struggling to move.

Boreal knelt down beside the creature. "Do not worry, my friend," he said soothingly. "You shall soon be free." Very carefully, he cut away the pieces of netting. "It looks like it has something stuck in its beak too," he added. "Probably a plastic bag."

Steph watched as the man removed pieces of plastic from the seagull's beak and couldn't help feeling guilty.

She was thinking about the bag that Noah had sent flying into the air. *I should have stopped him,* she thought.

When he'd finished, the old man carried the seagull into the waves and let it go. He and Steph stood in silence for a moment, watching as it dived beneath the surface.

"Will it be all right?" asked Steph.

Boreal looked at her, his expression unreadable.

"Who can say?" he said. "Come on … there is something else I want you to see."

Steph let out a long sigh as they turned. Then she saw it.

At the top of the beach stood an old building. Steph recognised it right away. She ran across the sand towards it.

"This is Mr Arnold's place," she cried when she got there. "The Sand Dune Café. This is where Mum works."

"No longer," Boreal told her. "When people stopped coming to the beach, the café had to close."

The door was boarded up but Steph managed to peer in through a broken window. Inside, it was filthy.

Thick layers of dust covered the tables and a stack of chairs stood against one wall. The floor was littered with rubbish.

"Is this what you wanted me to see?" asked Steph sadly.

"No," Boreal replied, as the twisting sands rose around them once again. "This is nothing."

Chapter 5

Wasteland

This time, the whirling cloud of sand didn't settle at their feet like it had done before. It was blown away by a dry, burning wind. The heat was terrible, but the smell was worse.

"Yuk!" cried Steph, cupping one hand over her nose and mouth. "What's that awful smell?"

Boreal looked at her sadly. "It is the smell of a dying planet," he said. "But do not worry, it is not your fault, or so you seem to believe."

"Where are we?" asked Steph. She didn't recognise anything at all.

It looked as though they were standing in the middle of a vast rubbish dump. There were mountains of rubbish all around them.

A loud rumbling noise made Steph look round.

She'd expected to see a large vehicle driving towards them, but what she saw took her by surprise. It might have been some kind of aircraft or even a spaceship. She'd never seen anything quite like it before.

As the huge craft flew over their heads, it opened its cargo doors. With a deafening crash, more rubbish fell to the ground, adding to the landscape of refuse around them.

"You still haven't told me where we are," shouted Steph, covering her ears.

Again, Boreal didn't answer. "Come on," he said, leading the way. As they walked, Steph realised they were walking over rubbish. There was no grass, sand or soil beneath their feet ... it was all rubbish.

Boreal led Steph up one of the mountains of rubbish.

Once at the top, they stopped and looked around.

"This place is awful," said Steph.

Not far away were the remains of an old town or village.

The ground was brown and dry, with not a tree or blade of grass in sight.

"It looks like a desert," said Steph.

"It is," said Boreal. "Without the sea there is no rain, and it has not rained here for years."

Boreal reached down to pick something up. "Look!" he said, holding it out to Steph.

"A bottle," mumbled Steph. "It looks just like the one I was going to throw."

Boreal nodded. "You wanted to know where we are," he said. "We have been in the same place all along."

"You mean this is what will happen in the future?" asked Steph.

"That will be up to you," said Boreal, "and the rest of humankind."

"But it's not … " Steph began, but somehow, saying it wasn't her fault didn't seem right anymore.

Boreal raised his arm to throw the bottle away, but Steph stopped him.

"Why should I not throw it when others do?" asked Boreal. "It is only one bottle."

"Let me have it," said Steph, reaching out to snatch the bottle from Boreal's hand.

27

As soon as the bottle touched her fingers, everything changed. Steph could hear the sea and the sound of children laughing again. There was no sign of Boreal anywhere.

"Well ... what are you waiting for?" said a voice behind her. It was Natalie, standing with her hands on her hips.

"Are you going to throw it or not?" she asked.

"No," Steph replied, looking at the bottle. "I'm going to put it in the bin."

"But it's only one bottle," said Natalie.

Steph shook her head. "It's never only one bottle," she said. "Imagine if everybody left one on the beach."

Steph turned and headed back towards the Sand Dune Café. Amir ran to catch up with her. "You're probably not interested," he said, "but I'm helping Mum and Dad do a beach clean tomorrow. It's just picking up rubbish, but it's quite good fun."

"That sounds cool," replied Steph. "I'll be here."

Just before going inside the café, she looked around to see if she could see the bearded old man on the beach.

There was no sign of him, but where he'd been working there was a huge figure made from driftwood and bits of rubbish. It had a long beard made of seaweed.

"I think that's supposed to be Neptune," said Amir, following her gaze.

"I think it's Boreal," replied Steph, with a smile. "He's watching over the beach, protecting it for tomorrow. And I think he might need our help …"

Things to think about

1. Do you think that Steph is good at accepting responsibility at the start of the story?
2. What did you think of the old man Boreal when you first met him in the story?
3. Do you think Amir and Steph feel the same way as their friends about throwing rubbish on the beach?
4. How does your impression of Boreal change as the story goes on?
5. How do you think Steph has changed by the end of the story?

Write it yourself

Some of the themes in this story are caring for our environment, taking responsibility, magic, respect and friendship. Choose one, or more, of these themes and try to write your own story.
Plan your story before you begin to write it.
Start off with a story map:
• a beginning to introduce the characters and where and when your story is set (the setting);
• a problem which the main characters will need to fix in the story;
• an ending where the problems are resolved.
Get writing! Try to include dialogue to show what your characters are like, and how they feel, for example:
"Oh, just ignore him," said Noah, sneering.

Notes for parents and carers

Independent reading
The aim of independent reading is to read this book with ease. This series is designed to provide an opportunity for your child to read for pleasure and enjoyment. These notes are written for you to help your child make the most of this book.

About the book
Steph is at the beach with her friends, and there is an old man making a statue out of driftwood and rubbish nearby. Her friends are littering the beach and the old man is cross with them. Just as Steph is about to litter the beach too, the old man takes her on a journey to see what damage this can do.

Before reading
Ask your child why they have selected this book. Look at the title and blurb together. What do they think it will be about? Do they think they will like it?

During reading
Encourage your child to read independently. If they get stuck on a longer word, remind them that they can find syllable chunks that can be sounded out from left to right. They can also read on in the sentence and think about what would make sense.

After reading
Support comprehension by talking about the story. What happened?
Then help your child think about the messages in the book that go beyond the story, using the questions on the page opposite. Give your child a chance to respond to the story, asking:
Did you enjoy the story and why? Who was your favourite character?
What was your favourite part? What did you expect to happen at the end?

Franklin Watts
First published in Great Britain in 2019
by The Watts Publishing Group

Copyright © The Watts Publishing Group 2019
All rights reserved.

Series Editors: Jackie Hamley and Melanie Palmer
Series Advisors: Dr Sue Bodman and Glen Franklin
Series Designer: Peter Scoulding

A CIP catalogue record for this book is
available from the British Library.

ISBN 978 1 4451 6529 5 (hbk)
ISBN 978 1 4451 6530 1 (pbk)
ISBN 978 1 4451 6984 2 (library ebook)

Printed in China

Franklin Watts
An imprint of
Hachette Children's Group
Part of The Watts Publishing Group
Carmelite House
50 Victoria Embankment
London EC4Y 0DZ

An Hachette UK Company
www.hachette.co.uk

www.franklinwatts.co.uk